Thomas C. McGoldrick

A Life of Cardinal Newman

Thomas C. McGoldrick

A Life of Cardinal Newman

ISBN/EAN: 9783337272838

Printed in Europe, USA, Canada, Australia, Japan

Cover: Foto ©Raphael Reischuk / pixelio.de

More available books at **www.hansebooks.com**

A LIFE

OF

CARDINAL NEWMAN.

BY

REV. THOMAS C. McGOLDRICK.

✠

BOSTON:
FLYNN & MAHONY,
1899.

To his Fellow-Assistants,

Rev. Michael H. Geary and Florence J. Halloran,

his dearest and truest friends,

this little volume is affectionately dedicated

by the Author.

St. Peter's Church,
    Dorchester, Mass.

ACKNOWLEDGMENT.

In the preparation of this biography, I have gleaned from all the standard lives of Cardinal Newman, but for the chief facts of his career I am indebted to an article which appeared in the columns of the "Liverpool Catholic Times."

LIFE OF CARDINAL NEWMAN.

THE lives of all great men are themes of undying fascination. The starry course of their example is a light to our feet and a lamp unto our paths. If even the material world about us is a teacher of the highest truths,

> "If every bird that sings,
> And every flower that stars the elastic sod,
> And every breath the radiant summer brings
> To the pure spirit is a Word of God,"

how deep and how sublime must the messages be which speak to us from the outspread pages of a noble human life! Man responsive to the divinity within him is a light from heaven; he is the great high priest of nature, giving articulate voice to the beauty, wonder and music of creation, and in the pathway of his glorified and inspiring life humanity toils ever onward and upward the towering hills of ideal manhood. Such leaders in the world's history are few. "Like stars, single and bright, they shine in the night. They break out in sudden loveliness like fair flowers amid the common grass. Alone they seem, and separate, and yet they are ours. Their gifts shed honor upon all. Separate, high, wonderful souls! they are the salt of the earth; they preserve mankind, its dignity, its purity and its tone. By them standards are upheld, banners are lifted, trumpets are blown, men's hearts are moulded, lives are transfigured, souls are thrilled."

On the very summit of true greatness I place the great religious teachers of the Catholic Church, because they have been possessed of the noblest ideals and have devoted all the energies of their lives to their realization for the welfare of their fellow-beings. "The world could do without great heroes, even without great discoverers; it cannot do without these saints of God." The world's models of true greatness are often misleading. It has often placed the diadem of glory on the brow of the tyrant who has built his throne upon the broken hearts of the people; it has often thrown the pall of oblivion over the guilty deeds of the conqueror and, because of his successful brutality, has called him great. But when the Church places her seal of approval upon a man, we may look upon him as a crown and a flower of the human race.

As I throw open the pages of history and see marching before me from far and near, from the depths of ages and the tribes and peoples of men, the saints and sages who have fought and bled in the cause of truth, I behold, walking side by side with Peter and Paul, Augustine and Bernard, Aquinas and Ignatius, radiant and serene, the face and figure of John Henry Newman, whose genius and whose holiness have enkindled a fire of truth in the heart of England which shall not be quenched forever.

His name is the highest and brightest which gleams upon the literary and religious horizon of this great century, and his life and career have excited a deep and increasing interest. Catholics and Protestants alike have delighted to make him the subject of their pens, while men differing on all other topics have met on the common ground of admiration for his genius and virtue. "The man was so indubitably honest," says one of his latest biographers, "so simple-natured and above the smallest prevarication, that when he put his pen to paper all Protestants wanted to read, because they knew he believed what he said."

PART I.

NEWMAN'S LIFE BEFORE HIS CONVERSION.

John Henry Newman, son of Mr. John Newman, was born in London, February 21, 1801, and was one of a family of six children. During the early part of his childhood Newman lived with his father in Bloomsbury Square, and it is not a little remarkable that one of his early playmates, as in after years his sincere friend, should have been Benjamin Disraeli, the famous Prime Minister of England. Newman grew up a sensitive, imaginative boy. He relates in his "Apologia" that the first book which influenced his childhood was the Bible — and I may remark in passing that the Bible has been the stepping-stone to greatness of nearly all the great men of Christendom. "It fired the eloquence of Chrysostom and Augustine. It inspired· the pictures of Fra Angelico and Raphael, and the music of Handel and Mozart." It was the theme of the immortal songs of Dante and Milton, and it led Newman by devious but ever-brightening ways to the bosom of the Catholic Church. His parents belonged to the evangelical section of the established Church; and, as his mother, Jemima Fourdrinier, was the descendant of Huguenots, his early religious teaching was tinged with Calvinism. But his mind was dreamy and reverent. He believed that the world was full of invisible spirits, and he never ventured alone in the dark without having first taken the precaution of crossing himself. He never could explain from whence he had derived this practice, for no one had ever spoken to him on the Catholic religion, which he knew at that time only by name. Once, it is true, his father, anxious to listen to a noble piece of music, took the child to a Catholic chapel, but all that the little fellow carried away was the remembrance of a pulpit and a preacher and a boy swinging incense. When Dr. Newman, at the zenith of his fame as a preacher, was living at Littlemore, near Oxford, and pondering his future course, he stumbled one day upon a tattered old schoolbook, which, he discovered, contained a rude drawing by his own hand. The picture represented, to quote his own words, "the figure of a solid cross upright, and next to it what may indeed be meant for a necklace, but what I cannot make out to be anything else than a set of beads with a cross attached." From the significant manner in which Dr. Newman refers to this trivial incident, it is plain that he regarded it at the time almost in the light of a prophetic intimation of his future career. Here, then, at ten years of age, Dr. Newman points us to the mystical beginnings of that grace by which he was led through Calvinistic Evangelicism and High Churchism to complete adhesion to the Catholic Church.

Newman graduated from Oxford in 1820. So brilliant were his attainments that in 1827, besides being vice-principal of one of the college halls, he was appointed an examiner for the degree of Bachelor of Arts, an honor rarely conferred on one so young. The year following he was made vicar of St. Mary's, at Oxford, and passed by rapid strides to the forefront of the religious life at the University. His influence rapidly spread and, long before he himself was at all conscious of the fact, others saw the signs of an incipient party in the enthusiastic and devoted homage of his friends, the first article of whose creed was belief in Newman.

During this time, though he never suspected it, Divine Providence was preparing him for his great life-work. Every noble life implies a period of probation and development. "Those who are familiar with tropical forests tell us that for months they look sombre and monotonous, till, suddenly, on some day they will rush into crimson blossom and blaze in masses of floral splendor under the noonday sun; but the glory so seemingly instantaneous is in reality a lengthened work, and the sun and wind and rain and the rich air and the glowing sky, — nay, even the lost promise and fallen leaves of many a previous season must have lent their influence for years together before the issue of them can stand there manifest in the eyes of wondering men." And so it is everywhere. Man does not spring into immediate possession of his powers in any of the possible acquisitions before him. It is first the little taking hold, then the larger grasp, till finally the full powers of the man are expanded to express the capacities of his soul for the reception of the fuller truth. And so Newman's life was moulded, rounded and perfected by myriad influences. His conversion was a growth. Let us mark his steps as he marched towards the vestibule of truth. Up to the age of twenty his spiritual equipment was scanty. At that time the Triune God and himself were the only two beings he recognized upon earth, and his desire was to do God's will, cost what it might. This belief in God went before him like the pillar of fire and cloud. Christ was the Light of the world, bringing an answer to the eager questions of the human soul. But where was Christ's truth? Not in the Bible only, for the Bible itself declared that Christ had established a church with authority to bind the consciences of men and with the power of infallibility to lead men across the darksome passes of error into the light of the eternal day. Where was this truth to be found, in which church? He asked this question as he communed with God in prayer; he asked it as he walked amid the wonders of creation; he sought its answer in the dusty tomes of Oxford libraries. The pursuit of it became the sovereign passion of his life. For a time he seemed to find it in the Anglican Church. The University of Oxford was at this time the home of Liberalism, that baleful creed which begins by teaching that one religion is as good as another and ends by proclaiming that no religion is best of all. License of thought, the natural outgrowth of Luther's principle of private judgment, was gradually eliminating the fundamental doctrine of Christianity. "Newman and his friends believed they had a mission, and its object was to prove the Apostolic descent of the Church of England, and to rouse men from their tepid and unreal profession of Christianity." To disseminate their views, they began the publication of a series of tracts for the *Times*. The tracts had no agreement except on one point, — all believed they would give the Roman Church a death-blow in England. Newman's belief was that the reformers were in greater error than the Church of Rome. The reformers changed the doctrine of authority, eliminated the Real Presence, degraded marriage with divorce, and stole away the safeguards of wedded love. They asserted the total depravity of man, denied freewill, ignored the symbolism of human nature and scouted the sacramental system. The Roman Church kept these great truths safely in her bosom, and yet he believed she had been corrupted, — believed it, as he afterwards confessed, on the false arguments of his teachers. In his search for truth his appeal was to antiquity; but, unfortunately, antiquity proclaimed the very doctrine which the Anglican Church condemned. How could he surmount this insurmountable difficulty? He would reform the Church of England and establish a middle way between Romanism and Protestantism. He would explain away the Thirty-nine Articles. For this purpose, he wrote the tract numbered XC. Jennings, in his "Life of Newman," says of it, "The tract caused a tremendous sensation. It was full of popery." Canon Oakley says that Tract XC. had not been out many days before Oxford was in a fever of excitement. "It was bought with such avidity that the very presses were taxed almost beyond their powers to meet the exigencies of the demand. Edition followed edition, by days rather than by weeks; and it was not very long before Mr. Newman, as I have heard, realized money enough by the sale of this shilling pamphlet to purchase a valuable library. If, during the month which followed its appearance, you had happened to enter any common room in Oxford between the hours of six and nine in the evening, you would have been safe to hear some ten or twenty voices eloquent on the subject of Tract XC. If you happened to pass two heads of houses or tutors of colleges strolling down High Street in the afternoon, or returning from their walk over Magdalen bridge, a thousand to one but you would have caught the words, 'Newman' and 'Tract XC.'" In the excitement, Newman retired to Littlemore to study more deeply. His faith in Anglican-ism was shaken completely. It was not the Apostolic

Church, because it denied the Apostolic doctrine. Where would he turn? What faith would appease the hunger of his heart? It seems as though he was allowed to wander through all the dark labyrinths of error to teach the world that peace of intellect cannot be found outside of the Catholic Church. She followed him like his shadow. It was she who was drawn from the bleeding heart of her Master on Good Friday. It was she who went forth on Pentecost armed with divine truth. It was she who stole upon the world, like strains of half-forgotten music, and awakened echoes that all the voices of the world could not stifle. It was she who, when heresy laid its degrading touch upon the Ark of Truth, hurled upon it the anathemas placed in her hands by the Son of God. It was she whose clarion notes warned the nations against Arius, Nestorius, Eutyches, Calvin, Luther, Henry VIII., and Voltaire. It was she who in every age bid defiance to earthly kings who by false promises strove to lure her to destruction, saying to them " Keep thy purple, O Cæsar! to-morrow they will bury thee in it, and we will sing over thee the ' De Profundis' and 'Alleluia,' which never change!" He saw her, when subjected to fierce persecutions, arising from them stronger and more beauteous than before. He heard her voice ringing out across the centuries, " Follow me! For nineteen centuries I have led humanity to the feet of God!" Side by side with the tumultuous procession of the world, he saw her sending down the pathway of the ages her increasing procession of saints and martyrs. He beheld her works of mercy, founded and maintained by her in numbers that astonish the world. And if, here and there in the revolving years, her feet were covered by the dust cast upon her by ungrateful children, was not her brow ever in the azure skies and did she not move among the stars of heaven? Yes: that was the Church of antiquity and the Church of the nineteenth century, to-day, yesterday and forever, "whose youth is renewed as the eagle's and underneath her the everlasting arms." "What is the use," said he, "of continuing this controversy or defending my position if, after all, I was forging arguments for Arius or Eutyches and turning devil's advocate against the much-enduring Athanasius and the majestic Leo? Be my soul with the saints and shall I lift up my hand against them? Sooner may my right hand forget its cunning and wither outright, as his who once stretched it out against a prophet of God. Anathema to a whole tribe of Cranmers, Ridleys, Latimers! Perish the names of Bramhall, Usher, Taylor, and Barrow from the face of the earth, ere I should do aught but fall at their feet in love and worship whose image was continually before my eyes, and whose musical words were ever in my ears and upon my tongue."

The end had arrived. Amid the tumult of doubt his Master had come to him, as He once came to the Apostle Peter. Let me recall that scene. It was the fourth watch of the night, and the disciples were on the stormy sea of Galilee, dashed from wave to wave. Peering through the darkness and the storm, they saw a figure, as of a spirit, moving over the waters. Peter, with characteristic ardor, cried out, "If it be thou, Lord, command me to come to thee"; and the figure answered, "Come," and Peter walked upon the waters; but, as the tempest was high, he feared and began to sink. But the Lord rebuked him, saying, "Why hast thou doubted, O thou of little faith?" Inspired by these words, he walked fearlessly with the Lord to the boat, and when they entered it Peter, falling at the feet of Christ, exclaimed, "Indeed, thou art the Son of God." And so it was with John Henry Newman. He saw the light upon the waters. Strange doubts and new emotions agitated his soul, and the cry went up from his heart, "If it be Thou, Lord, command me to come upon the trembling waters of doubt and through the dense darkness of the night"; and the voice of the ages answered, "Come." Newman hesitated, but the voice rang out again, "Come," and Newman walked upon the waters and entered the bark of Peter, which is the Church of Christ; and, standing in the sanctuary, he cried, "Thou art the Spouse of Christ."

Part II.

Newman's Life after his Conversion.

On the 8th of October, 1845, at the mature age of forty-four, the irrevocable step was taken. Father Dominic, a Passionist, "accepted his abjuration and reconciled him with the Mother Church, baptizing him under solemn conditions, and comforting him with the Holy Eucharist."

Newman's departure from the Church of England was an act of heroism. It was the surrender, from a human standpoint, of all the world holds most dear. The world's hero is surrounded by the world's applause; and it is relatively easy to face even the cannon's hot and murderous breath, when shouting thousands cheer us on — but to do the right deed and say the right word, hated and jeered by the multitude, and sneered at by friends of one's own household, and to give up all for conscience' sake, surely that is heroism of the highest type. Vehemence and abuse were showered upon him. "It was rumored that he was mad. It was publicly stated that he had quarrelled with the authorities at Rome, and had been suspended. Sermons were preached about him, pamphlets were written, lectures were delivered, and every good Protestant fulminated against him." Yes: Newman had left them and had been ordained a Catholic priest. Newman, the master of science, the possessor of a stupendous intellect, the man who knew the Protestant systems better than his fellows, had sought a refuge in the Church of Rome. He had gone from them, and no man in all England could utter a word against his moral character. " He craved for ideals of life more like the early Church," and " to our shame " says Canon Farrar, " he found, or he thought he found, the ideals more real in the Church of Rome, which he joined, than in the Church of England, which he left." Had he remained with them, even as a layman, he might have reached the most exalted heights . of fame. Such were the varied and rare endowments of his mind, that he might have been a poet-laureate, or a Lord Chancellor, or even a Protestant Archbishop of Canterbury; he might have been England's first composer, its finest musician, its best novelist or historian or leader of modern thought. He had turned his back on all and joined himself to the Roman Catholics, a body of Christians the least numerous and most despised in all England. Yes: John Henry Newman had the spirit of a martyr and a hero, and the call of his Master, and the burden of his Master's cross, were dearer to him than all the honors England could shower at his feet. At the time of his conversion, the Catholic Church in England was practically dead. Here is his own picture of it: " No longer the Catholic Church in this country; nay, no longer, I may say, a

Catholic community, but a few adherents of the Old Religion, moving silently and sorrowfully about as memorials of what had been. 'The Roman Catholics,' — not a sect, not even an interest, as men conceived of it; not a body, however small, representative of the Great Communion abroad, — but a mere handful of individuals, who might be counted, like the pebbles and detritus of the great deluge, and who, forsooth, merely happened to retain a creed which in its day, indeed, was the profession of a Church. Here, a set of poor Irishmen, coming and going at harvest time, or a colony of them lodged in a miserable quarter of the vast metropolis; there, perhaps, an elderly person seen walking in the streets, grave and solitary, and strange though noble in bearing, and said to be of good family and a 'Roman Catholic'; an old-fashioned house of gloomy appearance, closed in with high walls, with an iron gate, and yews, and the report attaching to it that 'Roman Catholics' lived there — but who they were and what they did, or what was meant by calling them Roman Catholics, no one could tell, though it had an unpleasant sound, and told of form and superstition."

But the Almighty, who guides the march of human history, was preparing a field for his vast talents. Five years after his conversion the Catholic hierarchy of England was re-established. The last bishop of the old hierarchy died in 1584. The first of the new ones was appointed in 1850.

The attitude of the English people with regard to this event is so vividly portrayed by Kathleen O'Meara in her "Life of Bishop Thomas Grant," that I borrow the entire description.

"It was not to be expected that an event so unlooked for and pregnant with such mighty consequences as the reorganiza-

tion of the Catholic hierarchy in England would pass without
evoking strenuous opposition and much angry remonstrance,
but even those who were prepared for the worst were aston-
ished at the depth of hostile feeling which it aroused in this
country. If the decree, which came forth from the Vatican as
softly ' as the whispering of a gentle air,' had been a threat of
foreign invasion, it could scarcely have aroused wider and more
general resentment than that which hailed the arrival of the
twelve mitred warriors who landed on our shores, intent on
conquest not of this world. All classes, from the highest to the
lowest, were united in indignation and alarm and vehement
resolve not to submit to the outrage which had been put upon
them. The *Times* struck the key-note of the concert. Com-
menting on the Cardinal's pastoral, it declared that the English
government and people were not going to tolerate ' this new-
fangled Archbishop of Westminster, on whom the title of
Cardinal had been conferred . . . it was a clumsy joke,
one of the grossest acts of folly and impertinence which the
Court of Rome had ventured to commit since the Crown and
the people of England had thrown off its yoke. . . . The
absurdity of the selection of this title for this illegitimate
prelate was equal to its arrogance. Everybody knew that
Westminster never was, in early Christian times, a bishop's
see, but a monastery, . . . it was a mere figment of the
papal brain . . . .' So thundered Jupiter on October 14,
in the year 1850.

" The *Times* having once struck the key-note, all the minor
satellites took it up and thundered in chorus against the ' papal
aggression.'

" The Anglican bishops petitioned the Queen ' to discountenance by all constitutional means the claims and usurpations of the Church of Rome.' The clergy, in turn, petitioned their bishops, and the bishops addressed their clergy to the same end. John Bull was not slow to follow the example thus set him in high places. He vented his feelings and proclaimed his orthodoxy after the usual manner. He lighted stakes on commons and in market-places, and consigned the pope and the cardinal and the whole paraphernalia of the Scarlet Lady to the flames; he blew trumpets and rang bells, church bells heading the chimes, and let off rockets and made processions by torchlight, in which thousands of loyal citizens marched in rank and file to the inspiriting sounds of the national anthem or 'The Rogues' March,' the choral harmony being rather sustained than impaired by a running-fire chorus of 'No popery!' from the most enthusiastic amongst the throng. 'No popery!' was the cry of the hour. It came from walls and doors and shop windows; the very stones echoed the cry, for small boys forsook the delights of marbles and tops to join in the service, and scrawled the magic words, 'No popery!' on the flagstones. The Oratorian Fathers came in for a lion's share of the general obloquy. 'We are cursed in the street,' says Father Faber, 'Even gentlemen shout from their carriage-windows at us.' If on this, as on another great national occasion, England expected every man to do his duty, she was not disappointed.

"Nor can we reasonably be surprised at such a universal lifting up of 'the voices of the floods.' The event which called it out was a wonder such as the world had only witnessed once before. It was the rolling away of the stone from the sepulchre, and the coming forth of the dead. As Christ had returned to life after His three days' sleep in the tomb, so now His mystic spouse, the Church, had broken her death-sleep of three hundred years, and arisen and come back to life. It was a vision well calculated to fill with terror all who beheld it not with the rejoicing eyes of faith. The sleeper whom her murderers had accounted dead was in the midst of them once more, not 'bound hand and foot with grave clothes,' but strong, serene, and beautiful as one whom death had never touched ; an angel in shining garments, she stood in the awful dawn-light of the resurrection, radiant with the eternal youth of immortality."

Of the first Provincial Synod, Miss O'Meara, in the work already quoted, gives us this description :

" In the month of July, 1852, the first Provincial Synod of Westminster was held at Oscott. The bishops and the clergy, reinvested with their long-lost rights, gathered together as in the olden times to legislate for the spiritual wants of their people. There were the Archbishop and twelve suffragans with their theologians, the delegates from thirteen newly erected chapters, the heads of religious orders, the rectors of ecclesiastical colleges, and the officials of the councils. It was one of those hours which it is given to communities, like men, to live but once in a lifetime. But solemn and overpowering as were the emotions of that hour, they found a voice to give them utterance. Dr. Newman, in that glorious outburst of Catholic joy and faith entitled ' Second Spring,' which poured from his own heart into the hearts of his assembled brethren, expressed, as adequately as human speech might do, the feelings that filled the Synod. After telling the oft-told tale of sorrow and death and persecution which his hearers knew so well, the orator imagines the spirit of one of the grand confessors of the nearer martyr times looking out into the future and beholding the spectacle that Oscott presented that day, thus addressing those around him : ' I see a bleak mount looking upon an open country, over against that huge town to whose inhabitants Catholicism is of so little account. I see the ground marked out, and plantations are rising there, clothing and circling the space. And there, on that high spot, far from the haunts of men, yet in the very centre of the island, a large edifice, or rather pile of edifices, appears, with. many fronts and courts, and long cloisters and corridors, and story upon story. And there it rises under the invocation of that same sweet and powerful name which has been our consolation in this valley. I listen, and I hear the sound of voices, grave and musical, renewing the old chant with which Augustine greeted Ethelbert, in the free air upon the Kentish strand. It comes from a long procession, and it winds along the cloisters —priests and religious, theologians from the schools, and canons from the cathedral, walk in due precedence. And then there comes a vision of well-nigh twelve mitred heads, and last I see a prince of the Church, in the royal dye of empire and of martyrdom, a pledge to us from Rome of Rome's unwearied love, a token that that goodly company is firm in apostolic faith and hope. And the shadow of the saints is there; St. Benedict is there, speaking to us by the voice of bishop and of priest, and counting over the long ages through which he has prayed and studied and labored. There, too, is St. Dominick's white wool, which no blemish can impair, no stain can dim ; and if St. Bernard be not there, it is only that his absence may make him be remembered more. And the princely patriarch, St. Ignatius, too, the St. George of the modern world, with his chivalrous lance run through his writhing foe ; he, too, sheds his blessings upon that train. And others, also, his equals or his juniors in history, whose pictures are above our altars, or soon shall be, the surest proof that the Lord's arm has not waxen short, nor his mercy failed, — they, too, are looking down from their thrones on high upon the throng. And so that high company moves on into the holy place, and there, with august rite and awful sacrifice, inaugurates the great act which brings it thither.' So ends the vision. Then the preacher asks : 'What is that act? It is the first Synod of a new hierarchy. It is the resurrection of the Church.' As the voice went on, tears flowed unrestrainedly on every side, till there was not a dry eye in 'that high company.'

" ' All were weeping,' said one of the canons from the cathedral, whom the seer had apostrophized in his vision, ' most of us silently, but some audibly. As to the big-hearted Cardinal, he fairly gave up the effort at dignity and self-control, and sobbed like a child.' The gentle preacher himself was so completely overcome, that it was with difficulty he was able to continue his discourse to the end. When it was over, Dr. Manning took him by the arm and led him away to his own room."

In 1849 he became superior of the Oratory in Alcester Street, Birmingham, preaching the first sermon there on the Feast of the Purification. This period of Newman's career is marked by a touching incident. In 1850 the cholera was raging at Bilston, in the black country, and, the health of the local priest having broken down, Bishop Ullathorne, of Birmingham, wrote to the superior of the Oratory, inviting his assistance. Unwilling to lay on others a duty he did not share himself, Father Newman, with his inseparable friend, Father Ambrose St. John, brought the consolations of their religion to the stricken Catholics. These two men, accustomed to the refinement of Oxford academic life, went about like ministering spirits among the poor and the afflicted, shedding sunshine on darkened homes, lifting up bruised hearts, helping the helpless, and whispering words of cheer into cheerless hearts.

It was not, however, as a missionary that Newman was to do his great work for the Church and the cause of God, but with the wizard power of his incomparable pen. "No other man," says a recent writer, "in this century has attained such a supreme mastery over the English tongue. It was to him an instrument of which he knew all the mysterious capabilities, all the hidden sweetness, all the latent power, and it responded with marvelous precision to his every touch, the boldest or the slightest. Persuasive winningness, scathing denunciation, vivid irony, convincing logic, soul-subduing pathos, graceful fancies, — all were at his command and came forth to do his bidding."

In the year 1850 he began a series of lectures on the present position of Catholics in England. They depicted the fanaticism and bigotry of Protestantism. A writer in a famous English literary publication, the *Speaker*, says of this object, "It was nothing less than this, — to roll back the great Protestant tradition of the court, the law, of society and literature ; to remove whole mountains of prejudice ; to cleanse the Protestant mind of all the slimy traces of slanders ; to shiver in pieces the prejudices of centuries, and to let the old faith of Englishmen stand forth as a body of doctrine and rule of life, which, though possibly false, nay, even dangerous, is yet not demonstrably founded upon the corruption of man's heart, or directly responsible for every crime in the calendar. What a task! Protestants though we are, we can scarcely forbear to cheer. The mastery displayed by Dr. Newman in grappling with it is beyond praise and without precedent. He is all that Burke is, and genuinely playful besides. He successfully conceals the prodigious effort he is making and the enormous importance of the verdict for which he is striving. An abler book it would be impossible to name."

About this time there arrived on the scene a new warrior for the cause of Protestantism, a converted priest, Dr. Achilli. He came from Italy to regale Protestant ears with the old calumnies about the confessional and the Inquisition. He was a man of vile character. It is remarkable that when Protestants want to know what the Catholic Church is, they should pin their faith to some unfortunate creature who has been ejected from her bosom with all the vehemence with which St. Paul shook the viper from his hand. "If we want to know what a rose is, we do not judge it by some withering and cankered specimen, with the insects crawling over its decay and the worms gnawing at its roots, and if we want to see what man is, we do not judge him by the pale and blighted victim of his own basest appetites. We little judge of men by the liar and the debauchee and of women by the slattern or the fallen. We judge men and women in the ideal of what they might be, in the pure and good and by what is purest and best in our own hearts." Why, then, should Protestants judge us by the cockle in our fold, and close their eyes to the radiant constellations of Saints, whose light in every age has illuminated the whole firmament, and whose heroic holiness has transfigured the face of the earth. The history of Achilli was well known, and Newman in these lectures. held him up to the scorn of mankind. A libel suit was the result. Bigotry was too intense to hope for a fair verdict, and Newman was fined one hundred pounds. The Protestant historian, Jennings, says, "The atmosphere of the whole proceedings was clouded with theological prejudice. The judge himself 'thanked God' that there was no Inquisition in England, or ever likely to be one; and the applause evoked by this extra-judicial utterance passed without any rebuke."

Impartial men, accustomed to weigh evidence, felt satisfied that the verdict involved a grave miscarriage of justice. Even the *Times*, notwithstanding its Protestant leanings, spoke out strongly, and declared "that the result of the trial would deal a terrible blow to the administration of justice in England, and that Roman Catholics would have good cause for the future to assert that here there is no justice for them, whenever litigation turns on a cause which arouses the Protestant passions of judges and juries."

In 1864 Canon Kingsley, in an article in *Macmillan's Magazine*, was unfortunate enough to commit himself to the following statement: "Truth for its own sake has never been a virtue with the Roman clergy. Father Newman informs us that it need not be, and on the whole ought not to be." Stung to the quick at such an amazing misrepresentation, Newman, whose whole life had been a struggle for truth, rose like a Samson to crush his malicious adversary. He wrote to the publishers, "not," as he said, "to expostulate or to seek reparation, but to draw their attention as gentlemen to a grave and gratuitous slander with which, he felt confident, they would be sorry to find their names associated." Kingsley, in a general way, refused to retract. He must have forgotten when he did so that he recklessly threw down a defiance to the most skilful controversialist of his age and the greatest living master of the English tongue. Newman, in a series of letters, smote and spared not.

Here is Newman's analysis of the correspondence between himself and Mr. Kingsley:

Mr. Kingsley begins then by exclaiming: "Oh the chicanery, the wholesale fraud, the vile hypocrisy, the conscience-killing tyranny of Rome! We have not far to seek for an evidence of it. There's Father Newman to wit: one living specimen is worth a hundred dead ones. He, a priest, writing of priests, tells us that lying is never any harm."

I interpose: "You are taking a most extraordinary liberty with my name. If I have said this, tell me when and where."

Mr. Kingsley replies: "You said it, Reverend Sir, in a sermon which you preached, when a Protestant, as Vicar of St. Mary's, and published in 1844; and I could read you a very salutary lecture on the effects which that sermon had at the time on my opinion of you."

I make answer: "Oh . . . Not, it seems, as a priest speaking of priests;—but let us have the passage."

Mr. Kingsley relaxes: "Do you know, I like your tone. From your tone I rejoice, greatly rejoice, to be able to believe that you did not mean what you said."

I rejoin: "Mean it! I maintain I never said it, whether as a Protestant or as a Catholic."

Mr. Kingsley replies: "I waive that point."

I object: "Is it possible? What, waive the main question? I either said it or I did n't. You have made a monstrous charge against me, — direct, distinct, public. You are bound to prove it as directly, distinctly, as publicly, or to own you can't."

"Well," says Mr. Kingsley, "if you are quite sure you did not say it, I 'll take your word for it; I really will."

My word! I am dumb. Somehow I thought that it was my word that happened to be on trial. The word of a professor of lying, that he does not lie!

But Mr. Kingsley reassures me: "We are both gentlemen," he says; "I have done as much as one English gentleman can expect from another."

I begin to see: he thought me a gentleman at the very time he said I taught lying on system. After all, it is not I, but it is Mr. Kingsley who did not mean what he said. *Habemus confitentem reum.*"

So we have confessedly come round to this, preaching without practising,— the common theme of satirists from Juvenal to Walter Scott. " I left Baby Charles and Steenie laying his duty before him," says King James of the reprobate Dalgarno. " O Georgie, jingling Georgie, it was grand to hear Baby Charles laying down the guilt of dissimulation, and Steenie lecturing on the turpitude of incontinence."

But Kingsley was not generous enough to admit his guilt. He repeated his unfounded assertions and endeavored to prove that " Dr. Newman's whole career had been one long tissue of double dealing." In order to place himself in the right position before the public and posterity, Dr. Newman wrote the " Apologia pro Vita Sua."

"The 'Apologia,'" says Fletcher's "Life of Newman,"

"appeared in weekly numbers, being published on seven successive Thursdays in the summer of 1864. Before the second
part issued from the press, the whole of religious and educated
England was filled with an interest that bordered on excitement. The successive parts were waited for with eagerness,
and men found a wonderful charm in watching, as it were, the
unfolding of a soul before their eyes. The magnificent English
of the book, the fascinating style, attracted and charmed.
In presence of so wonderful a production, the controversy with
Canon Kingsley was forgotten, and men began to recognize
the fact that in Newman England possessed one of her greatest
and most wonderful sons. A great revulsion of feeling set in
amongst all classes. The name of John Henry Newman
began to be mentioned everywhere with respect and love; it
was felt that in him Christianity possessed one of its doughtiest
champions and most sterling examples of practical piety.
Without ever seeming egotistical, he showed men, in the
'Apologia,' how truth had been the one guiding star of his
existence, leading him on step by step, until it had brought him
into what he firmly and unquestionably believed to be the one
true fold of Christ.

"The effect of the publication of the 'Apologia' was to
bring upon him a perfect avalanche of congratulatory
addresses from all parts of the world. Diocesan chapters,
friendly societies, foreign ecclesiastical congresses, bishops,
academies, religious societies, — all took advantage of the
opportunity to present him with assurances of their affection
and regard. His own bishop, the late Dr. Ullathorne,
addressed to him a long letter, full of admiration for his life
and work. An address reached him from far-away Hobart

Town, and another from our colonies in Australia. It seemed as though men could not do enough to show their esteem for one whose character, at length, stood forever beyond suspicion."

It may be of interest to my readers to know the opinion of Newman's character and intellectual attainments entertained by some of his eminent Protestant contemporaries. I quote, first, a tribute paid to him by James Anthony Froude, in *Good Words:*—

"When I entered at Oxford, John Henry Newman was beginning to be famous. The responsible authorities were watching him with anxiety; clever men were looking with interest and curiosity on the apparition among them of one of those persons of indisputable genius who was likely to make a mark upon his time. His appearance was striking. He was above the middle height, slight and spare. His head was large, his face remarkably like that of Julius Cæsar. The forehead, the shape of the ears and nose, were almost the same. The lines of the mouth were very peculiar, and I should say exactly the same. I have often thought of the resemblance, and believed that it extended to the temperament. In both there was an original force of character which refused to be moulded by circumstances, which was to make its own way, and become a power in the world; a clearness of intellectual perception, a disdain for conventionalities, a temper imperious and wilful, but along with it a most attaching gentleness, sweetness, singleness of heart and purpose. Both were formed by nature to command others, both had the faculty of attracting to themselves the passionate devotion of their friends and followers; and in both cases, too, perhaps the devotion was rather due to the personal ascendency of the leader than to the cause which he represented. It was Cæsar, not the principle of the empire, which overthrew Pompey and the constitution. *Credo in Newmannum* was a common phrase at Oxford, and is still unconsciously the faith of nine-tenths of the English converts to Rome.

"It has been said that men of letters are either much less or much greater than their writings. Cleverness, and the skilful use of other people's thoughts, produce works which take us in till we see the authors, and then we are disenchanted. A man of genius, on the other hand, is a spring in which there is always more behind than flows from it. The painting or the poem is but a part of him inadequately realized, and his nature expresses itself, with equal or fuller completeness, in his life, his conversation, and personal presence. This was eminently true of Newman. Greatly as his poetry had struck me, he was himself all that the poetry was, and something far beyond. I had then never seen so impressive a person. I met him now and then in private; I attended his church and heard him preach Sunday after Sunday. He is supposed to have been insidious, to have led his disciples on to conclusions to which he designed to bring them, while his purpose was carefully veiled. He was, on the contrary, the most transparent of men. He told us what he believed to be true. He did not know where it would carry him. No one, who has ever risen to any great height in this world, refuses to move till he knows where he is going. He is impelled in each step which he takes by a force within himself. He satisfies himself only that the step is a right one, and he leaves the rest to Providence. Newman's mind was world-wide. He was interested in everything which was going on in science, in politics, in literature. Nothing was too large for him, nothing too trivial, if it threw light upon the central question, what man really was, and what was his destiny. He was careless about his personal prospects. He had no ambition to make a career, or to rise to rank and power. Still less had pleasure any seductions for him. His natural temperament was bright and light; his senses, even the commonest, were exceptionally delicate."

Mr. R. H. Hutton, who, in the *English Leaders of Religion*, has written a very interesting life of Newman, speaks of him in the following eulogistic terms : —

" I suppose that one may safely regard it as a standard of true greatness to surpass other men of the same calibre of culture and character, men with whom comparison is reasonable, in the ardor and success with which any purpose worthy of the highest endeavor is prosecuted. Measuring by this standard, it would be hard to fix on any man now living in England who could rival Cardinal Newman in the singleness, the devotion, the steadfastness, and the nobility of his main effort in life. I say this, though I cannot adopt for myself his later conception of the Church of Christ, hardly even that earlier conception which led so inevitably to the later. But that is nothing to the purpose. What is perfectly clear to any one who can appreciate Cardinal Newman at all, is that, from the beginning to the end of his career, he has been penetrated by a fervent love of God, a fervent gratitude for the Christian revelation, and a steadfast resolve to devote the whole force of a singularly powerful and even intense character to the endeavor to promote the conversion of his fellow-countrymen from their tepid and unreal profession of Christianity to a new and profound faith in it, which new and profound faith in it could, in his belief, be gained only by the reorganization of the Christian Church, and its re-enthronement in a position of authority even greater than that which it held in the middle ages."

Lewis E. Gates, the present professor of English in Harvard University, concludes a sympathetic criticism of Newman as follows: "Though he is rarely, if ever, so ornate as De Quincey, and though he perhaps never weaves his prose into such a lustrous, shining surface through the continual use of sensations and images as does De Quincey in his impassioned prose, yet the glowing beauty, the picture-making power, the occasional imaginative splendor, the elaborate swelling music of Newman's writings, place him as a master of prose in the same group with De Quincey, and Ruskin, and Carlyle, and part him from Landor, or Macaulay, or Matthew Arnold. No prose can more surely send quivering over the nerves a sense of the shadowing mystery of life, than certain of Newman's sermons, and passages here and there in his 'Apologia' and in his 'Essays.' Through the play, then, of his imagination, its rhythms and beat of the wing, because of the ease with which in a moment his prose can carry the reader into regions of impassioned and mystical feeling, even because of the vital, intimate warmth and color of his phrasing, — qualities so different from the hard, external glitter of Macaulay's specific, but rhetorical style, — Newman reveals his kinship with the great group of poets and prose-writers who deepened and enriched the imaginative life of the early part of our century."

And yet, amid all this fierce controversy, Dr. Newman

attended to his parish work at Egbaston. The sermons he preached there are the most elaborate specimens of his eloquence. "They represent," says Hutton, "the full-blown blossom of his genius, while his Oxford Protestant discourses represent it in its bud." With regard to these sermons there is a striking story told in the *Catholic World.* The writer of the article paid a visit to Dr. Newman, and while at the Oratory he made a remark about the lack of education of the Birmingham congregation, suggesting that Dr. Newman, in preaching such exquisite sermons, was throwing his pearls before swine. This roused Dr. Newman, who saw the sonship of God shining ever under the dust of the gutter child, and he responded, with a deep intensity of feeling, " There may be pearls, but there are no swine. I can take you into the poorest district of this parish and show you as noble a heart beneath the frock of a smith as ever throbbed in the bosom of an English lord."

As an example of his exquisite style and the tenderness of his heart, read this story of Magdalen, taken from his "Sermons to Mixed Congregations " : —

" It was a formal banquet, given by a rich Pharisee, to honor, yet to try, our Lord. Magdalen came, young and beautiful, and ' rejoicing in her youth,' ' walking in the ways of her heart and the gaze of her eyes ' : she came as if to honor that feast, as women were wont to honor such festive doings, with her sweet odors and cool ungents for the foreheads and hair of the guests. And he, the proud Pharisee, suffered her to come, so that she touched not him; let her come as we might suffer inferior animals to enter our apartments without caring for them ; perhaps suffered her as a necessary embellishment of the entertainment, yet as having no soul, or as destined to perdition, but anyhow as nothing to him. He, proud being, and his brethren like him, might 'compass sea and land to make one proselyte,' but as to looking into that proselyte's heart, pitying its sin, and trying to heal it, this did not enter into the circuit of his thoughts. No: he thought only of the necessities of his banquet, and he let her come to do her part, such as it was, careless what her life was, so that she did that part well and confined herself to it. But, lo, a wondrous sight! was it a sudden inspiration or a mature resolve? Was it an act of the moment or the result of a long conflict? — but behold, that poor, many-colored child of guilt approaches to crown with her sweet ointment the head of Him to whom the feast was given; and she has stayed her hand. She has looked, and she discerns the Immaculate, the Virgin's Son, 'the brightness of the Eternal Light, and the spotless mirror of God's majesty.' She looks, and she recognizes the Ancient of Days, the Lord of life and death, her Judge; and again she looks, and she sees in His face and in His mien a beauty and a sweetness, awful, serene, majestic, more than that of the sons of men, which paled all the splendor of that festive room. Again she looks, timidly yet eagerly, and she discerns in His eye and in His smile the loving-kindness, the tenderness, the compassion, the mercy of the Saviour of man. She looks at herself, and oh, how vile, how hideous is she, who but now was so vain of her attractions! How withered is that comeliness, of which the praises ran through the mouths of her admirers! How loathsome has become the breath, which heretofore she thought so fragrant, savoring only of those seven bad spirits which dwell within her! And there she would have stayed, there she would have sunk on the earth, wrapped in her confusion and in her despair, had she not cast one glance again on that all-loving, all-forgiving countenance. He is looking at her; it is the Shepherd looking at the lost sheep, and the lost sheep surrenders herself to Him. He speaks not, but He eyes her, and she draws nearer to Him. Rejoice, ye angels! she draws near, seeing nothing but Him, and caring neither for the scorn of the proud nor the jests of the profligate. She draws near, not knowing whether she shall be saved or not, not knowing whether she shall be received or what will become of her; this only knowing, that He is the Fount of holiness and truth, as of mercy, and to whom should she go but to Him who hath the words of eternal life? 'Destruction is thine own, O Israel; in me only is thy help. Return unto me, and I will not turn away my face from thee: for I am holy and will not be angry forever.' 'Behold, we come unto thee; for thou art the Lord our God. Truly the hills are false, and the multitude of the mountains. Truly the Lord our God is the salvation of Israel.' Wonderful meeting between what was most base and what is most pure! Those wanton hands, those polluted lips, have touched, have kissed the feet of the Eternal, and He shrank not from the homage. And as she hung over them, and as she moistened them from her full eyes, how did her love for One so great, yet so gentle, wax vehement within her, lighting up a flame which was never to die from that moment, even forever! and what excess did it reach, when He recorded before all men her forgiveness and the cause of it! 'Many sins are forgiven her, for she loved much; but to whom less is forgiven, the same loveth less. And he said unto her, Thy sins are forgiven thee; thy faith has made thee safe, go in peace.'"

Where can we find a more powerful presentation of the Catholic doctrine of the Atonement than in his sermon "on the mental sufferings of our Lord in His passion"?

"There, then, in that most awful hour, knelt the Saviour of the world, putting off the defences of His divinity, dismissing His reluctant angels, who in myriads were ready at His call, and opening His arms, baring His breast, sinless as He was, to the assault of His foe, — of a foe whose breath was a pestilence and whose embrace was an agony. There He knelt, motionless and still, while the vile and horrible fiend clad His spirit in a robe steeped in all that is hateful and heinous in human crime, which clung close round His heart, and filled His conscience, and found its way into every sense and pore of His mind, and spread over Him a moral leprosy, till He almost felt Himself to be that which He never could be, and which His foe would fain have made Him. Oh, the horror, when he looked and did not know Himself and felt as a foul and loathsome sinner, from His vivid perception of that mass of corruption which poured over His head and ran down even to the skirts of His garments! Oh, the distraction when He found His eyes, and hands, and feet, and lips, and heart, as if the members of the Evil One and not of God! Are these the hands of the Immaculate Lamb of God, once innocent, but now red with ten thousand barbarous deeds of blood? Are these His lips, not uttering prayer, and praises, and holy blessings, but as if defiled with oaths, and blasphemies, and doctrines of devils? or His eyes, profaned as they are by all the evil visions and idolatrous fascinations for which men have abandoned their adorable Creator? And His ears, they ring with sounds of revelry and of strife; and His heart is frozen

with avarice, and cruelty, and unbelief; and His very memory
is laden with every sin which has been committed since the
fall, in all regions of the earth, with the pride of the old giants,
and the lusts of the five cities, and the obduracy of Egypt,
and the ambition of Babel, and the unthankfulness and scorn
of Israel.   Oh, who does not know the misery of a haunting
thought which comes again and again, in spite of rejection, to
annoy, if it cannot seduce? or of some odious and sickening
imagination, in no sense one's own, but forced upon the mind
from without? or of evil knowledge, gained with or without
a man's fault, but which he would give a great price to be rid
of at once and forever?   And adversaries such as these gather
around Thee, Blessed Lord, in millions now; they come in
troops more numerous than the locust or the palmer-worm, or
the plagues of hail, and flies, and frogs which were sent
against Pharaoh.   Of the living and of the dead and of the as
yet unborn, of the lost and of the saved, of Thy people and
of strangers, of sinners and of saints, all sins are there.   Thy
dearest are there, Thy saints and Thy chosen are upon Thee;
Thy three Apostles, Peter, James and John; but not as com-
forters, but as accusers, like the friends of Job, 'sprinkling
dust towards heaven,' and heaping curses on Thy head.   All
are there but one; one only is not there, one only; for she
who had no part in sin, she only could console Thee, and
therefore she is not nigh.   She will be near Thee on the Cross;
she is separated from Thee in the garden.   She has been Thy
companion and Thy confidant through Thy life; she inter-
changed with Thee the pure thoughts and holy meditations of
thirty years: but her virgin ear may not take in, nor may her
immaculate heart conceive, what now is in vision before Thee.

None was equal to the weight but God. Sometimes before Thy saints Thou hast brought the image of a single sin, as it appears in the light of Thy countenance, or of venial sins, not mortal; and they have told us that the sight did all but kill them, nay, would have killed them, had it not been instantly withdrawn.

" The Mother of God, for all her sanctity, nay, by reason of it, could not have borne even one brood of that innumerable progeny of Satan which now compasses Thee about. It is the long history of a world, and God alone can bear the load of it. Hopes blighted, vows broken, lights quenched, warnings scorned, opportunities lost, the innocent betrayed, the young hardened, the penitent relapsing, the just overcome, the aged failing, the sophistry of misbelief, the wilfulness of passion, the obduracy of pride, the tyranny of habit, the canker of remorse, the wasting fever of care, the anguish of shame, the pining of disappointment, the sickness of despair ; such cruel, such pitiable spectacles, such heartrending, revolting, detestable, maddening scenes, nay, the haggard faces, the convulsed lips, the flushed cheek, the dark brows of the willing slaves of evil,— they are all before Him now; they are upon Him and in Him. They are with Him instead of that ineffable peace which has inhabited His soul since the moment of His conception. They are upon Him, they are all but His own; He cries to His Father as if He were the criminal, not the victim; His agony takes the form of guilt and compunction. He is doing penance ; He is making confession; He is exercising contrition, with a reality and a virtue infinitely greater than that of all saints and penitents together : for He is the One Victim for us all, the sole Satisfaction, the real Penitent, all but the real sinner."

When he speaks of the Blessed Virgin it is with a reverence and sweetness of a St. Bernard. I will illustrate this by a single passage from his sermon "On the Fitness of the Glories of Mary":—

"She died in private. It became Him, who died for the world, to die in the world's sight; it became the Great Sacrifice to be lifted up on high, as a light that could not be hid. But she, the lily of Eden, who had always dwelt out of the sight of man, fittingly did she die in the garden's shade, and amid the sweet flowers in which she had lived. Her departure made no noise in the world. The Church went about her common duties, preaching, converting, suffering. There were persecutions; there was fleeing from place to place; there were martyrs; there were triumphs. At length the rumor spread abroad that the Mother of God was no longer upon earth. Pilgrims went to and fro; they sought for her relics; but they found them not. Did she die at Ephesus? or did she die at Jerusalem? Reports varied; but her tomb could not be pointed out, or if it was found it was open, and instead of her pure and fragrant body, there was a growth of lilies from the earth which she had touched. So inquirers went home marvelling and waiting for further light. And then it was said, how that, when her dissolution was at hand, and her soul was to pass in triumph before the judgment-seat of her Son, the apostles were suddenly gathered together in the place, even in the Holy City, to bear part in the joyful ceremonial; how that they buried her with fitting rites; how that the third day, when they came to the tomb, they found it empty, and angelic choirs with their glad voices were heard singing day and night the glories of their risen Queen. But however we feel towards the details of this history (nor is there anything in it which will be unwelcome or difficult to piety), so much cannot be doubted, from the consent of the whole Catholic world and the revelations made to holy souls, that, as is befitting, she is, soul and body, with her Son and God in heaven, and that we are enabled to celebrate, not only her death, but her Assumption."

It would be quite impossible in these few pages to give an adequate estimate of Dr. Newman's writings. His most popular works, written since his conversion, are "Callista," "Loss and Gain," "Lectures on Anglican Difficulties," "Historical Essays," "The Present Position of Catholics in England," the "Apologia," "Meditations and Devotions," and the "Grammar of Assent." The contrast between the writings of Newman the Anglican and Newman the Catholic is very pronounced, and emphatically in favor of the Catholic. "It is like the meeting of great waters. The one restrained, at times uneasy, eminently unpopular, remote from the trodden paths of feeling; the other exuberant, though never redundant, triumphant, sometimes almost to the pitch of boisterousness, sweeps along, marshalling his forces, polishing his epigrams, and making his appeals no longer to the scholar and theologian and prim church-goer, but to the man in the street, — the rank and file of humanity." R. H. Hutton writes, "From the moment when Newman became a Roman Catholic the freest and happiest, though not perhaps the most fascinating, epoch of his life may be said to have commenced. I do n't know that he ever again displayed quite the same intensity of restrained and subdued passion as found expression in many of his Oxford sermons ; but, in irony, in humor, in eloquence, in imaginative force, the writings of the later, and, as we may call it, the emancipated portion of his career, far surpass the writings of his theological apprenticeship."

Newman was not only a great writer of prose, but he was also a poet of a high order. His first great poem was a prayer so sweet and so touching that it has become all over the world a favorite hymn with Protestants, as well as Catholics. It was while his mind was tortured with darkness and doubt and his soul craved for light, that he wrote the world-famous verses, "Lead, Kindly Light." Newman was on the Mediterranean, returning home after a long voyage and a severe illness. One evening, when the afterglow of the sunset was deepening into gloom, he sat upon the deck of the vessel, asking the never-ceasing questions of the human soul. He seemed alone with the sea and the sky and the stars, and they spoke to him of God in a language all their own. And, lo! with the dying twilight, sky and sea and stars faded from his view, and he knelt on the altar-stairs of nature, that slope up through the darkness; and there, submissive to the divine will, this exquisite hymn welled up from his heart: —

> Lead, kindly Light, amid th' encircling gloom;
> Lead Thou me on!
> The night is dark, and I am far from home;
> Lead Thou me on!
> Keep Thou my feet; I do not ask to see
> The distant scene; one step enough for me.
>
> I was not ever thus, nor pray'd that Thou
> Shouldst lead me on;
> I loved to choose and see my path; but now
> Lead Thou me on!
> I loved the garish day, and spite of fears,
> Pride ruled my will. Remember not past years!

So long Thy pow'r hath bless'd me, sure it still
    Will lead me on;
O'er moor and fen, o'er crag and torrent, till
    The night is gone !
And with the morn those angel faces smile
Which I have loved long since, and lost a while !

His most scholarly and longest poem is "The Dream of Gerontius." It is a sublime picture of a soul's passage from time into eternity. In vivid touches Newman paints the terrible scenes which intervene between the soul and the judgment-seat of God. Gerontius beholds the fallen hosts of Satan, who are hungering for his soul. He listens to their discordant cries and asks for information about them. The angel makes answer to him : —

    " That sullen howl
Is from the demons who assemble there.
It is the middle region, where of old
Satan appeared among the sons of God,
To cast his jibes and scoffs at holy Job.
So now, his legions throng the vestibule ;
Hungry and wild, to claim their property,
And gather souls for hell.   Hist to their cry !

   .   .   .   .

It is the restless panting of their being;
Like beasts of prey, who, caged within their bars,
In a deep hideous purring, have their life,
And an incessant pacing to and fro."

As the soul is led by its guardian angel unfalteringly over heaven's azure, it dashes away, in the intemperate zeal of its love, from its heavenly guide to the feet of God. It has dared to gaze at the "Light inaccessible," before which the seraphim veil their eyes with awe and the cherubim grow mute with an ecstacy of love; and, blinded by its own unworthiness, it falls

back, scorched and shrivelled. Filled with a sense of its
sinfulness, it begs to be carried to the Purgatorial flames :—

> " Take me away, and in the lowest deep,
>   There let me be ;
> And there in hope the lone night watches keep
>   Told out for me.
> There, motionless and happy in my pain,
>   Lone, not forlorn,
> There will I sing my sad perpetual strain,
>   Until the morn.
> There will I sing and soothe my stricken breast,
>   Which ne'er can cease
> To throb and pine, and languish, till possest
>   Of its Sole Peace.
> There will I sing my absent Lord and Love.
>   Take me away,
> That sooner I may rise and go above,
> And see Him in the truth of everlasting day."

The evening of Newman's life was as calm and beautiful as
the setting of a summer sun. The happy community life in
the Oratory at Birmingham is described by W. S. Lilly, in the
Fortnightly Review : —

" In order fully to appreciate Dr. Newman, it was necessary
to be with him in his own home, among the devoted fathers
and brethren with whom his life was passed. His mornings
were usually sacred to his work ; but in the afternoon, at the
period of which I am speaking, he would take a long walk —
he was still a great pedestrian — in which his visitor had the
privilege of accompanying him. At six o'clock the community
dinner took place ; and, on the days when his turn came
round, ' the father ' would pin on the apron of service and wait
upon his brethren and his visitor, — who, to say the truth, was

somewhat uncomfortable in being thus ministered to — not himself sitting down until they had received their portions. All ate in silence, broken only by the voice of the lector, who, from a pulpit in the corner, read first a few verses from the Vulgate, then a chapter of the life of a saint, and, lastly, a portion from some modern work of general interest. When dinner was over, questions in some department of theological science were proposed by one of the community. Each of the fathers, in succession, gave his opinion, ending with the formula, 'But I speak under correction.' Then the proposer summed up. After that, we all adjourned for 'recreation' to a neighboring parlor, where coffee was served and the pent-up flood of conversation burst forth, — the play of wit and fancy, the wealth of anecdote and reminiscence, the tender glances at the past, the keen remarks upon events of the day, in all of which Father Newman would fully bear his part, not more at home in his graver pursuits than in this genial hour, which recalled to me the description given of the first Oratory, presided over by St. Philip Neri himself, 'the school of Christian mirth.' Some portion of the evening Dr. Newman would, not unfrequently, devote to music. I suppose we are all familiar with that passage in his 'Oxford University Sermons,' in which 'the mysterious stirrings of heart and keen emotions, and strange yearnings after we know not what, and awful impressions, we know not whence,' are described in words whose majestic eloquence, I think, has never been surpassed. He who wrote thus of music, was himself no mean performer upon the violin."

On April 12, 1879, Pope Leo XIII., who recognizes and rewards merit wherever he finds it, raised Father Newman to the dignity of a Cardinal Prince of the Church, and the whole world, Catholic and Protestant, rejoiced in the honors conferred upon him.

It was on Monday, August 11, 1890, at the age of ninety, that the heart of the greatest preacher and writer' of the century throbbed on to the great silence, and Newman was at rest forever. At his tomb the jeers of a quarter of a century ago gave place to a unanimous outburst of admiration and reverence from all the English churches and all the English sects.

> With ninety golden years to crown his life,
> And soul undimmed by cruel hate or strife,
> The prince of England's priests has sunk to rest;
> The warrior sleeps upon his Saviour's breast.
>
> Around his tomb the world has gathered now,
> To place its grateful wreaths upon his brow;
> And England mourns, with all a mother's tears,
> Her noblest son, the wisest of her seers.
>
> Supremest master of his native tongue,
> A poet sweet as e'er in numbers sung, —
> He knew the subtlest workings of the mind;
> Its deepest depths his piercing gaze could find.
>
> Confessed by all as England's greatest sage,
> Whose wisdom speaks on every glowing page,
> He stands upon the lofty heights of fame;
> Their gleaming summits bear his magic name.
>
> Though kings must die and kingdoms pass away,
> And sculptured stone must crumble in decay,
> His songs shall live; his burning thoughts sublime
> Shall mock the crushing hand of cruel time.
>
> But gifts of mind were not his noblest part,
> For Christ-like deeds were born within his heart.
> He might have worn his country's laurel crown,
> Or 'mong her brilliant statesmen gained renown;

But higher aims and grander dreams had he,
Than worldlings' vulgar eyes can ever see.
No painted pomp could fire his noble breast;
No passing fame could give his spirit rest.

While round him surged the throng, allured with gold,
Or in ambition's vain pursuit cajoled,
He walked with God. His thoughts were fixed above,
Where angels sang of Christ's redeeming love;

And, lo! upon his ear their swelling strain
As softly fell as summer's gentlest rain.
Their music ruled his life, and urged his pen
To wake its chords within the hearts of men;

And, like the statue famed in ancient days,
Which sang when touched by morning's orient rays,
His regal soul, with fervent zeal ablaze,
Gave back his Master's gifts in hymns of praise.

And now the toiler sleeps, — his work is done,
His gentle life its saintly course hath run;
"And with the morn those angel faces smile,
Which he had loved long since, and lost a while."

Sleep on and rest, thou loyal priest of God,
Whose feet in duty's paths alone have trod !
Thy lyre is not unstrung, — its music o'er;
In mighty books it lives forevermore.

THE END.